A
Tale of
Two Shoes

By Helen Haraldsen

Illustrated by Steve Hutton

A Tale of Two Shoes

Editing and formatting by www.letsgetbooked.com

Illustrated by Steve Hutton

Hardback ISBN: 978-1-9160112-2-9

Paperback ISBN: 978-1-9160112-1-2

eBook ISBN: 978-1-9160112-0-5

This book is dedicated, with loving memory to Dorothy Hutton, mum,

who always believed in better. . .

Steve Hutton

One

Have you ever noticed those poor abandoned single shoes left in the strangest of places around the countryside? A trainer dangling by its laces from a telephone wire, a broken stiletto lying next to a gutter as rain soaks into it or a wellington boot standing alone on the pavement outside a shop, looking like it's waiting for the sale to begin?

How do they all get to be there? Where is their partner?

This is the story of two such shoes, cruelly separated by a toddler tantrum.

Shane and Sheila were a pair of glossy red buckled shoes. They started their life in a factory in China and had to endure a dark, rough journey across the sea until they ended up in a shoe shop in the north of England. Poor Shane Leftfoot remained packed away in the dark shoe box, but lucky Sheila Rightfoot was brought out and put on display amongst the other children's shoes. She missed Shane terribly as they had never been apart since their creation. However, she did make friends with Lacey Rightfoot – a polka dot lace-up, and Tracey Rightfoot - a bright white, Velcro trainer.

It wasn't long before Sheila found herself being plucked from her shelf and strapped to the right foot of a lively three-year-old girl. Much to her delight, Shane soon joined her and the pair of them were modelled in front of a ground level mirror.

"Look at those lovely shoes," a woman's voice said in a sing-song voice. "Do you like them?" The answer must have been yes as Shane and Sheila were soon unstrapped, wrapped up safely in their shoe box and taken away, ready to start their new life in the world.

They had many adventures attached to the feet of little Poppy Walker. Many were exciting, like skipping through fresh grass sprinkled with daisies or even jumping through crunchy autumn leaves, but some were horrible like getting plunged into muddy puddles (*oh Poppy! Look, now you've got your lovely red shoes all wet*) or stepping in squidgy piles that smelled revolting (*oh Poppy! Look where you're going*). But they loved that they were Poppy's favourite shoes and got to go everywhere she went.

It wasn't to last.

Two

Poppy started to grow, and although Shane and Sheila still fitted her, her shoe collection began to expand. Soon, Shane and Sheila found themselves being replaced as Poppy's favourites by newcomers: Wallace and Wendy, a pair of bright green wellingtons.

One day, Poppy wanted to wear her wellies, but her mum insisted she wore the red shoes as, "you can't wear green wellies with a pink dress, poppet."

Poppy pleaded and whined and cried but her mum was adamant. Shane and Sheila found themselves fastened to the feet of a writhing and protesting Poppy as she was strapped into the car, kicking and screaming.

In all the kerfuffle, Sheila hadn't been fastened properly, and unbeknown to her parents in the front seats, Poppy managed to pull Sheila off her right foot. Although it was March, it was a warm day with the sunlight streaming into the car. Poppy's mum – who was in the front passenger seat – put her window down to let some air in. As they pulled up at a red traffic light, Poppy saw her chance. She raised her little arm, and with all her three-year-old might, chucked poor Sheila shoe right out of the window. By the time Poppy's mum worked out what had happened, the light had changed to green, and the car had to drive away. Poor Sheila was left all alone in the gutter with an abandoned plastic bottle and a half-eaten pizza.

Sheila lay there all day, cold and alone. She hoped that Poppy's parents might come back for her, but as the sky darkened and it started to rain, she realised no-one was coming to her rescue.

Torrential rain lashed from the grey sky, and soon the gutter was filling with cold, dirty water. Sheila felt herself moving; she was being picked up and carried by the gushing water. Down the road she went, bumping into all the litter being swept along with her. Her prayers for the ordeal to be over were soon answered when a huge lorry hurtled past, its humongous wheels causing such an enormous splash that Sheila was lifted on the crest of the wave and sent flying over the wall into the field on the other side. She landed in a soggy cowpat and stayed there all night.

Three

Poppy and her parents had arrived back home. Poppy was in a bad mood as she'd had to attend a party wearing just one shoe and her parents were angry because one red shoe was no good to anyone. Poor Shane found himself being thrown in the bin with the potato peelings and empty crisp packets.

It seemed that Shane and Sheila would never meet again.

***

The morning after Sheila found herself being tossed into a cowpat, she was picked up and carried in the great slobbering mouth of a huge, yellow dog. She felt the dog's teeth digging into her and worried that they would mark her shiny red leather.

Fortunately for her, the dog's owner noticed when he came to put the slobbering beast on the lead. "What have you got there you silly boy?" Sheila heard a man say. "Put it down." But the dog didn't let go. Sheila was disgusted by the warm, wet saliva dribbling all over her, but before things could get any worse, she felt a hand close around her and she was released from the dog's grip. Sheila breathed a sigh of relief that she wasn't going to be eaten alive, before realising she was completely alone again. The man had looked around for a bin, but seeing none, he placed poor Sheila on a nearby wall and walked away, leaving Sheila all by herself.

Four

Back at Poppy's house, Shane was still in the bin. Presently, he felt himself being lifted into the air before slipping forwards and falling right into the huge open mouth of a hungry monster. The strange creature already had lots of rubbish in its mouth, but it kept stopping to pick up more. Shane cowered in fear as pile after pile was thrown on top of him.

Just when he thought he was about to be buried forever, Shane was falling again as the monster coughed him up with all the other rubbish. He found himself sitting on top of a stinking heap of junk, covered in bits of smelly, leftover food, which made him feel very unloved.

As he began to lose hope, Shane suddenly discovered he was flying. He soared through the air, watching the fields and roads pass underneath him. Soon he could smell the sea – he recognised the scent from when he'd been to the beach on Poppy's left foot.

Before long, Shane found himself in a nest of what looked like fluffy speckled stones. Shane realised they were baby birds – seagull chicks. An enormous adult seagull had swooped in and picked him up along with a beak full of food scraps from the tip before bringing him to her chicks for their lunch. Shane was pecked and prodded all over before the birds realised he could not be eaten.

Seeing no reason for this shoe to remain in her nest, the mother gull tossed him over the side. Shane bounced off the rocky cliff face, all the way to the bottom until he landed at last on soft brown sand. Phew, thought Shane. I'm glad I'm out of there. I'm safe now.

Little did Shane know, the tide was coming in.

Five

After hours of loneliness spent pining for Shane and Poppy, Sheila once again found herself with unwanted company. It was late in the afternoon and fewer people were on the streets. Out of nowhere, a large black cat appeared on the wall next to her. She had no idea where it had come from and its sudden silent appearance scared her.

"Alright?" It appeared the cat was speaking to her. Sheila was startled. She had never spoken to an animal before and hadn't even realised they could speak. She wasn't sure how to reply, so she said nothing. The cat came closer; its whiskers tickled as its big yellow eyes peered at her.

"I'm Bruno," said the cat, sitting down and looking at her expectantly. When she didn't respond, Bruno prompted her. "And you are...?"

"*Sh.-Sh.-Sheila*", she whispered forlornly.

"Why are you sitting here on this wall by yourself Sheila? Don't shoes always come in pairs?" Bruno purred, rubbing his head against her.

The cat's warmth and concern gave her the courage to speak. "*I've been separated from my partner and I'm lost!*" she sobbed.

"Oh noooo," Bruno purred again, sitting down on the wall, wrapping his long tail around Sheila. "Poor you. Shoes aren't like cats. You're meant to have company."

"*Yes, that's right,*" Sheila murmured, snuggling into the fluffy tail.

"I might be able to help you out. Stay there," he said before disappearing from sight, leaving Sheila feeling cold and frightened once again.

Just as she was starting to worry that she'd be spending the night all alone on the wall, Bruno returned. This time he was joined by a small tabby cat.

"Oh yes, I see," the tabby said. "She'll love it." And with no explanation, Sheila was abruptly travelling swiftly through the streets in the mouth of the tabby cat. Its teeth were smaller but sharper than the dog's teeth, and they prickled uncomfortably.

Minutes later, they approached a small house with a bright red front door that was similar to Sheila's colour. The cat entered the house through a flap in the door and Sheila immediately recognised where she was from the warmth and the smells that greeted her. She was in a kitchen. She knew it wasn't Poppy's house as it was smaller, and the cupboards were a different colour. Nevertheless, it felt welcoming and homely.

Sheila was delighted and wanted to thank the cat, who had now dropped her on the kitchen floor, but she didn't get the chance as a woman entered the room and the cat went straight to her, twisting itself around her legs.

"Ohhh, hello, there's my baby," the woman cooed, bending down to scoop up the cat and pressing it to her face. "And what have you brought me today then kitty?" She was looking down at the bedraggled red child's shoe on her kitchen floor. "A ruby slipper huh?" She scratched the cat behind its ears. "Have you brought Mummy a beautiful ruby slipper instead of a disgusting dead mouse? Who's a clever girl?"

The cat was returned to the floor and given a saucer of milk, while Sheila was picked up and given a lovely hot bubble bath in the sink. *Ahhh, this is more like it*, she thought to herself, even though she wondered why this lady seemed so pleased to be given a single shoe. As Bruno had said, shoes don't work on their own.

What was going to happen to her?

Six

While Sheila was enjoying her hot bubble bath, Shane was having a bath of his own – but it wasn't as pleasant. He'd been sitting on the sand at the bottom of the cliff watching seagulls circling above him, hoping they wouldn't poo on him, when he started to feel an unpleasant sensation. At first, he wasn't sure what it was, though he was sure he'd felt it before.

It was cold and it filled him up like the muddy puddle Polly had taken him and Sheila in to once. Shane was lifted up by the sea and carried on its current all through the night.

Days and nights passed, bobbing on the waves like a miniature red dinghy, until one morning, Shane found himself on a different beach. There were no cliffs there; the sand was pale yellow and sparkled in the early morning heat. Shane enjoyed basking peacefully in the sunshine until people started to come onto the beach. They brought towels and rugs and plastic buckets and spades and played in the sea.

No-one noticed Shane until much later in the day when a man nearly stood on him while walking barefoot in the sand. He reached down and picked Shane up. His face broke into a wide smile revealing dazzling white teeth and he exclaimed happily in a language Shane didn't understand. He found himself being placed into a bag the man was carrying, which contained an assortment of other items from the beach – sea smoothed glass and pebbles, sticks, plastic bottles and sections of netting. Shane wondered where this journey would take him.

Seven

It was a glorious sunny morning in England. Sheila was now completely clean and dry and looking forward to the day ahead. She was sure that things were going to improve. Maybe this nice lady would help her to find Shane and Poppy again.

After a bit of pottering about, drinking coffee and eating toast, the lady took Sheila out into her back garden. She was also carrying a hammer and a nail, which seemed a bit strange to Sheila. The garden was pretty and colourful, full of flowers, butterflies and bees. Birds were singing and the air smelled of spring. It was like paradise...until she noticed something strange about the large trees at the bottom of the garden. Nailed to almost every tree was a shoe. Sheila was horrified!

The lady took her to one of the trees and positioned her against a gently sloping branch. Then a nail was hammered into the sole to hold her in place. *Ow!* thought Sheila as she felt a brief stab of pain. It soon passed and she was able to take in her surroundings. On her right were two trees close to each other, which both had a boot nailed to them. She later learned that they were called Boris and Brenda. They used to be the lady's walking boots until their stitching had rotted and they started to leak. On her left was a purple trainer – this was Thomas. He used to have a partner – Teresa – but she'd been chewed to bits by the neighbour's dog before ending up in that dreaded place: the bin.

Sheila could not believe that Boris, Brenda and Thomas seemed quite happy about being nailed to a tree. She couldn't see anything to be pleased about. She was going to be stuck there forever; she'd never visit any exciting places; never find Shane again, and she'd get cold and wet. She'd never felt so forlorn.

"I can't bear this," she wailed. "I need to get back home! Poppy needs me. *Shane needs me...and I need them.*"

"You'll be needed here," Brenda boot told her. Sheila couldn't see how she could possibly be of any use while nailed to a tree, but it didn't take long for her to see that she was wrong.

Eight

On the other side of the world, Shane was no longer a piece of discarded rubbish in a carrier bag. He had become a piece of art – a sculpture. The man with the dark skin and white teeth wasn't just picking litter off the beach to clean it up, he was using what he'd found to create something beautiful and unique.

Just out of the reach of the waves, at the top of the beach, he was creating a sculpture that captured the grace and serenity of a sea turtle. Shane had been placed into the part making up the turtle's multicoloured shell – but that peaceful tranquillity was in contrast to the nets and plastic bags entangled around its body.

The sculpture had been made to show people how the turtles were becoming endangered at the hands of humans and the pollution they caused. Visitors came from all over to see the sculpture and read the information boards nearby. News crews came and filmed it, sending the story all over the world.

A lady in England saw it one night while drinking a cup of coffee with a tabby cat curled on her lap.

"Look at that kitty. Isn't that clever?" she said.

Even more people started to visit. Soon there were hundreds every day.

Shane was famous! He felt so proud and thankful to be a part of something so worthwhile. There were other shoes in the sculpture besides him. It took them a while to learn how to communicate with each other as they spoke different languages, but eventually, they found ways to understand each other.

At night, when the visitors left the beach and the sky turned dark, Shane would look up at the stars. Sometimes he would wonder what had happened to Sheila. He hoped she was as content as he was and that she had found some purpose, as he had, as a single shoe.

Nine

Sheila had indeed found her own special happiness in the back garden where she still remained. Not long after Brenda had told her she would be needed, Sheila had started to see what she meant. Small birds started to land in the garden. A couple of small brown birds headed straight for Brenda and began arranging twigs and bits of moss inside her. *"Ahh, welcome back my little family!"* she greeted them.

A few days later, another pair of birds started doing the same thing to Boris and Thomas. They seemed to have been expecting them and welcomed their arrival, as Brenda had. Sheila hadn't understood what was happening and felt nervous when a bird started showing an interest in her. It hopped around her, inspecting her from different angles then it called out in a high-pitched whistle. Soon its mate appeared and joined in with the survey. Before she knew it, the birds had moved in!

Sheila was lined with twigs and moss before the female bird promptly began laying eggs until there were four in the nest. The little eggs hatched into chicks and they remained with Sheila while the parent birds worked hard to find enough food to feed all the hungry mouths.

It seemed like little time had passed before the tiny chicks had grown. They teetered out onto the edge of the nest before stepping off and disappearing into the grass below, where their parents continued to feed them until they were old enough to fly away and start their lives.

Sheila was heartbroken when the baby birds left and didn't come back. She missed the feeling of them all snuggling together as they sheltered inside her; missed hearing their cheery cheeps. But most of all, she missed feeling wanted. Brenda noticed Sheila's unhappiness and knew just what to say to cheer her up. *"You're not alone Sheila. You'll never be alone again."* She was right: soon the female bird was back, laying more eggs and the whole process started again.

Then Sheila realised what Brenda had meant. She was needed in the most important way: she was a home, a safe place to raise a family, part of a community.

Eventually, all the birds left the nest for good.

"Don't worry," Brenda told her, "they'll be back next year."

Sheila didn't think she could wait a full year for her little family to return and was very distressed when the lady came and took all the abandoned nests away.

***

As the weather began to get colder and the days got shorter, the lady would come out and pour seed into Thomas and Sheila. All sorts of birds would drop in for a snack, and Sheila welcomed their company.

At night when all the birds were sleeping and she could see the stars through the bare branches, she sometimes thought about Shane. Although she had become good friends with Boris, Brenda, and Thomas, she still missed her companion. Sheila hoped that Shane was as happy as she was and had found a way to be useful once again.

Ten

Shane and Sheila never saw each other again. When they were first separated, they felt lonely and sad. They didn't think they could exist without each other. But they both learned that, in fact, they could. Shane enjoyed all the attention he got as well as the knowledge that he was part of something important – he was appreciated and special. Sheila didn't receive any fame or glory, but she was equally happy, year after year, seeing new lives raised within her – lives that she helped to shelter and protect.

So, if you ever find yourself on your own unexpectedly, just think of Shane and Sheila. Don't worry or panic or feel lonely. Look around you and seek out new friends, join in with another group, try something new, give things a chance. Sheila thought her world had ended when Poppy threw her out of the window, but it ended up being the best thing that ever happened to her.

And, of course, if you see someone who is feeling left out, lonely or worried, you could reach out to offer them comfort and support. Everyone needs a friend.

Life doesn't always go smoothly and sometimes things happen that aren't nice. But good things can come out of bad times and happiness can often be found in unexpected places. You just need to be prepared to look for it.

About the Author

Helen lives in Cumbria with her husband, horses and a variety of dogs, hens, ducks and geese! As well as writing books, she also teaches English and runs a secondary school library.

Visit www.helenharaldsen.co.uk to find out more about Helen and to sign up to the mailing list. You'll receive news, updates, opportunities and free, exclusive bonus material linked to HH Books.

Did you enjoy this book? The author would love to see your reviews on Amazon.Please feel free to post your comments and let others know about A Tale of Two Shoes.

Also by this Author

Amber's Pony Tales

For readers aged 8 -12

Coming Soon

The Dalmatian That Lost its Spots

For readers aged 5 – 8